**Butch**

*Miss Loopy*

# poochie-poo

# Poochie-Poo

## Helen Stephens

David Fickling Books

OXFORD · NEW YORK

Thankyou to David (person),
Maria (person), Ness (person)
and Victor (pooch).

A DAVID FICKLING BOOK

Published by David Fickling Books
an imprint of Random House Children's Books
a division of Random House, Inc.
1540 Broadway
New York, New York 10036

Published simultaneously in Canada by Random House of Canada Limited, Toronto. Originally published in Great Britain by David Fickling Books, an imprint of Random House Children's Books.

www.randomhouse.com/kids

Library of Congress Cataloging-in-Publication Data available upon request

ISBN 0-385-75012-9 (trade)—ISBN 0-385-75018-8 (lib. bdg.)

Printed in Singapore

July 2003

10 9 8 7 6 5 4 3 2 1

First American Edition

**Victor** is a well-behaved, lovable pup and he lives with *Miss Loopy.*

*Miss Loopy* adores **Victor**. She kisses him and cuddles him whenever she can. She buys him treats, and her favorite thing is to tickle him under his chin and say "Coo-chi-coo!" **Victor** loves being tickled and fussed over except . . .

. . . when his friend **Butch** comes to visit. **Butch** is a very small, very naughty pup. **Victor** thinks **Butch** is cool.

One day **Butch** came to visit. "You two pups play nicely," said *Miss Loopy.* "I'm not playing nicely," said **Butch**. "Let's play baddies." "Yes," said **Victor**. "Let's play baddies."

"Here are some doggy biscuits,
you two pups," said *Miss Loopy*.
"Delicious!" said **Victor**.

"Baddies don't eat
doggy biscuits,"
said **Butch**.
"They eat table legs!"

" Fetch my slippers, darling," said *Miss Loopy.* "Baddies don't fetch slippers," said **Butch**, "they hide them!"

"Good boy, coo-chi-coo!" said *Miss Loopy* and she tickled **Victor's** tummy.

"Baddies don't have their tummies tickled," said **Butch**, "they are too busy stealing sausages!"

"And another thing," said **Butch**, "Baddies aren't called **Victor**. They have names like Buster or Knuckles. You're a useless baddie!"

**Victor** felt very sad. He tried to think of a way to show **Butch** what a brilliant baddie he was.

Later that afternoon, when
*Miss Loopy* took them shopping,
**Victor** saw a sign that said:

"NO DOGS ALLOWED."
This gave **Victor** an idea . . .
and he told **Butch**.

"Watch this!" said **Victor**. "I'm going to run into that shop where it says "NO DOGS ALLOWED."

**Butch** was very impressed.
**Victor** ran into the shop . . .

. . .then straight back out
again! He felt terrible for
being so naughty so he
shouted to the shopkeeper,
"Sorry about that!"
"Baddies don't say sorry,"
said **Butch** and he
laughed at **Victor** all
the way home.

But **Victor** didn't care because he didn't want to be a baddie now. "I wasn't cut out for a life of crime," he said.

Suddenly the door bell rang. *Miss Loopy* opened the door and there stood *Miss Froopy-Frou-Frou.* "Hello, *Miss Froopy-Frou-Frou,*" said *Miss Loopy.* "Come in."

"Where is my darling pup?"
cried *Miss Froopy-Frou-Frou*.
"Come to Mummikins,
my little poochie-poo.
Have you missed me?
Come on, poochie-poochie-
poochie-poo!"
And *Miss Froopy-Frou-Frou*
picked up **Butch** and
tickled his tummy.

**Butch** blushed.

"Baddies don't blush!" said **Victor**.

"Bye, bye," said
*Miss Froopy-Frou-Frou.*
"Bye, bye,"
called *Miss
Loopy.*

"Bye, bye,
Poochie-poochie-
poochie-poo!"
said **Victor**.

Miss Froopy-Frou-Frou

Butch

Victor